THIS CANDLEWICK BOOK BELONGS TO:

A you're a-dor-a-ble B you're so beau-ti-ful C you're a cu-tie full of charms

D you're a dar-ling and E you're ex-cit-ing and F you're a feath-er in my arms

G you look good to me H you're so hea-ven-ly I you're the one I i-dol-ize

J we're like Jack and Jill K you're so kiss-a-ble L is the love-light in your eyes

Dedicated to the children of the world—they are all beautiful.
S.L., B.K., and F.W.

For Amy Ehrlich and David Ford, who came up with the idea in the first place. M.A.

Text copyright © 1994 by Aria Music Co. and Budd Music Corp.
Illustrations copyright © 1994 by Martha Alexander

Based on the song "'A'—You're Adorable," words and music by Buddy Kaye, Fred Wise, and Sidney Lippman; copyright © 1948, renewed 1976 by Aria Music Co. and Budd Music Corp. (ASCSAP)

First U.S. paperback edition 1996

The Library of Congress has cataloged the hardcover edition as follows:

Lippman, Sidney.
A you're adorable / words and music by Sidney Lippman, Buddy Kaye, and Fred Wise ; illustrated by Martha Alexander.—1st ed.

Summary: An assortment of children and pets climb over, under, and through the letters of the alphabet in this illustrated presentation of a familiar song. Includes music.
ISBN 1-56402-237-4 (hardcover)
1. Children's songs—Texts. [1. Alphabet. 2. Songs.] I. Kaye, Buddy.
II. Wise, Fred. III. Alexander, Martha G., ill. IV. Title.
PZ8.3.L635Yo 1994
[E]—dc20 93-931
ISBN 1-56402-566-7 (paperback)

10 9 8 7 6 5 4 3 2

Printed in Hong Kong

This book was typeset in Garamond ITC Book.
The pictures were done in watercolor.

Candlewick Press
2067 Massachusetts Avenue
Cambridge, Massachusetts 02140

A You're Adorable

Words and music by Buddy Kaye, Fred Wise, and Sidney Lippman

Illustrated by
Martha Alexander

CANDLEWICK PRESS
CAMBRIDGE, MASSACHUSETTS

you're adorable

you're so beautiful

you're a cutie
full of charms

D

you're a
darling and

you're
exciting
and

you're a
feather
in my arms

you look good to me

you're so heavenly

you're the
one I idolize

we're like
Jack and Jill

you're

so

kissable

L is the
   lovelight
      in your eyes

I could go on all day

alphabetically speaking, you're okay

made my

life complete

means you're
very sweet

It's fun to wander through

the alphabet with you

to tell you
what you mean
to me!

A you're a - dor - a - ble   B you're so beau-ti - ful C you're a cu-tie full of   charms

D you're a dar - ling and E you're ex - cit - ing and F you're a feath-er in   my   arms

G you look good to me H you're so hea-ven-ly   I you're the one I   i - dol-ize

J we're like Jack and Jill   K you're so kiss-a - ble L is the love - light in   your   eyes

M   N   O   P   I could go on — all day   Q   R

S   T   al - pha - bet - i - cally speak-ing you're o - kay — U made my life com-plete

V means you're ver - y sweet W—————— X Y Z— It's

fun to wan-der through the al-pha-bet with you to tell you what you mean to me!—

BUDDY KAYE, FRED WISE, and SIDNEY LIPPMAN are three world-famous songwriters. In addition to "A You're Adorable," they are individually responsible for Nat King Cole's "Too Young," Barry Manilow's "The Old Songs," and Perry Como's "Till the End of Time." Perry Como's recording of "A You're Adorable" has sold over three million copies.

MARTHA ALEXANDER has written and illustrated many children's books, including the Lily and Willy board books and *You're a Genius, Blackboard Bear.* She particularly enjoyed illustrating *A You're Adorable* because it gave her the chance "to include fun things that I wouldn't ordinarily do, such as my chickens and nonsense things." Mother of two, grandmother of eight, and great-grandmother of five, Martha Alexander lives in Hawaii.